Read other titles in the series

h2O

Just add
water!

1 No Ordinary Girl

2 Living With Secrets

3 Fishy Business

4 A Sleepover Tail

A Sleepover Tail

Adapted by Rachel Elliot

SIMON AND SCHUSTER

SIMON AND SCHUSTER
First published in Great Britain in 2009 by Simon & Schuster UK Ltd,
1st Floor, 222 Gray's Inn Road, London WC1X 8HB
A CBS Company
Originally published in Australia in 2007 by Parragon
Licenced by ZDF Enterprises GmbH, Mainz

A CIP catalogue record for this book is available from the British Library

ISBN 978-1-84738-540-6

10 9 8 7 6 5 4 3 2 1

Printed by CPI Cox & Wyman, Reading, Berkshire RG1 8EX

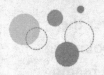
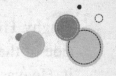

Chapter 1

In the vast, blue ocean just off the Gold Coast of Queensland, Mako Island lay silent and mysterious. It was a prehistoric-looking outcrop, surrounded by shark-filled reefs. Its steep slopes were covered with a thick canopy of trees and bushes, which made it look almost as if it was trying to hide. Even though the morning was bright and sunny, the tall, rocky cliffs and the looming volcano top looked dark and cold. Strange shadows played across the island's surface and a faint mist was wreathed around the highest point.

Not far from the island, a lonely dinghy was bobbing on the deep, blue water. Next to Mako Island, it looked like a white speck. There were no other boats around for miles, and the tiny dinghy looked very small and vulnerable.

Lewis McCartney was sitting alone in the

dinghy. His fishing line was dangling over the side of the vessel, but he wasn't even looking at it. He was absorbed in the book he was reading – *An Anthology of Mythical Sea Creatures* by Dr Sandra Holmes.

A short distance from the boat, *something* moved. *Something* was watching Lewis and getting closer.

Lewis turned a page, fascinated by the old-fashioned drawings of sea monsters and tall, rigged ships. *This is brilliant*, he thought. *All those centuries ago, people really knew about this stuff.*

The *something* drew closer and closer to the fragile little dinghy, hidden beneath the surface. Through the cool depths of the ocean, it made its way steadily towards the boat. For a moment, it broke the surface, watching the solitary boy as he fished and read. There was a long, silent pause.

Then suddenly, a phone rang.

Lewis put the book down on his lap and

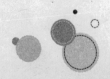

picked up the phone, which was lying on the seat next to him. Alerted by the ringing noise, the *something* slipped back underwater and charged straight towards the dinghy.

"Hello?" said Lewis.

There was a pause as he listened to the caller.

"Yeah, just a second," he said.

He held the phone out over the water.

"It's for you," he said, and the *something* shot through the surface of the water and took the phone.

It was a mermaid.

It was a young, blonde mermaid.

Lewis didn't bat an eyelid – he was used to it by now. She was his friend Emma Gilbert, and just like Rikki Chadwick and Cleo Sertori, she turned into a mermaid whenever she touched water. When he had first found out about their secret, Lewis had stared at his friends' tails in amazement, eager to watch them as they swam.

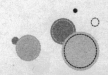

But by now he had seen it all before – he just picked up his book and carried on reading.

Lewis had bumped into Emma early that morning as she was heading down to the beach for a swim. Neither Rikki nor Cleo had been answering their phones, so Emma was pleased to see Lewis. He had been planning a morning of fishing, and they agreed to head out to sea together. Emma had made Lewis laugh by darting around his boat at jet speed, flicking water at him with her tail. They had stopped just off Mako Island and Emma had gone to explore the reefs while Lewis read his book and waited for the fish to bite.

Emma put the phone gingerly to her ear, trying not to get it too wet.

"So have you decided what time for the party tonight?" said Cleo's excited voice in her ear.

Emma sighed. *How many times do I have to tell her that there's not going to be any party?* she thought. She repeated the words that she

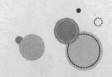

had said to Cleo at least twenty times already. There was no way she was going to hold a party when the tiniest drop of water could turn her into a mermaid. Not a chance. People would be rushing around, carrying drinks, not paying attention to where they were going or what they were doing. It was just too risky.

"Emma, this is a tradition we're talking about!" said Cleo in an exasperated voice.

"I know," said Emma, as patiently as she could. "But I just don't see how I can have the party this year. Not with … recent developments."

She flicked her tail in the water and glanced up at Lewis, who grinned at her. *Surely she can understand why this is so difficult?* Emma thought. *How can I have a party when I have this huge secret? Being a mermaid makes life difficult enough without adding more danger!*

Emma listened as Cleo chattered on, trying to persuade her to change her mind. Then a frown wrinkled her forehead and a worried

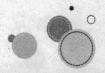

expression came into her eyes.

"Your new job?" she repeated, looking up at Lewis to get his attention. "The dolphin tank? At the Marine Park?"

"The *what*?" said Lewis, appalled. He let the book slip to the bottom of the dinghy as he and Emma stared at each other in horror. What was Cleo *thinking*?

Back on shore, Cleo was putting fish into a bucket, ready to feed to the dolphins. She rolled her eyes as Emma's words poured into her ear, warning her about the dangers of a job like that and growing more and more high pitched.

"Yes, of *course* the tank's full of water, Emma," said Cleo, as if Emma was being very stupid. "They're aquatic mammals."

She continued picking up fish and dropping them into the bucket as she listened to Emma arguing with her. Cleo's expression grew a little more stubborn.

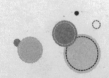

"Yes, I do remember what water does to me," she said. "But I'm not going to let that run my life."

Cleo's supervisor, Mrs Geddes, walked into the room and saw her on the phone. She frowned and tried to catch Cleo's eye, but Cleo was too busy arguing to notice.

"Look, Emma, I really want to make this work," Cleo said, trying to explain herself.

I can't just put my life on hold because of this, she thought. *I always wanted to work at the Marine Park, and I've been on the waiting list for ages! Now I've finally got a job here, there's no way I'm giving it up!*

"*Cleo?*" said Mrs Geddes, meaningfully.

"I've got to go," said Cleo, cutting Emma off and putting her phone down.

She picked up a floral shower cap and fitted it over her head. She was already wearing a full-length waterproof apron, waterproof gloves and galoshes. A thick towel was tucked into the back of her apron.

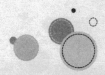

"Cleo … are you all right?" asked Mrs Geddes in an uncertain tone.

"Yep!" said Cleo. "Ready when you are."

She picked up the buckets that she had filled with dead fish and squid, plopping one last fish into it with a pair of tongs. Then she followed Mrs Geddes out to the dolphin pool, carrying one heavy bucket in each hand. Her heart thumped in excitement – she was actually going to feed the dolphins! Cleo loved all animals, and being able to help them and care for them was a dream come true.

She stopped by the edge of the water and watched as the two dolphins raced over to her. They poked their heads eagerly out of the water. Cleo put the buckets down and laughed as she looked at them. *I love this job*, she thought. *I just hope that I can make Emma understand how much this means to me.*

She began to toss fish into the dolphins' mouths, and they clicked and squealed in delight.

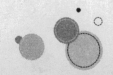

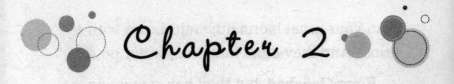

Chapter 2

Meanwhile, Emma was still hanging on to the edge of the dinghy, staring at her phone in disbelief. *Cleo hung up on me!* she thought. *She actually hung up on me!*

"She can be so stubborn sometimes," she said, handing the phone back to Lewis.

Lewis didn't reply. Secretly, he admired Cleo for standing up for herself to Emma. *It's about time she showed everyone how amazing she is,* he thought. *I'm just not so sure that working in the Marine Park is the best way for her to do it.*

He put the phone down on the seat next to him and picked up his book again, opening it at a page featuring a medieval-looking mermaid. Emma peered at it doubtfully.

"So, do you really think that's going to tell us something useful?" she enquired.

"It's already told me you guys are hotter

than your usual mermaid," said Lewis with a grin. "And they don't have cool water powers."

Emma laughed, but then her expression grew serious.

"There's only one place we're going to find answers to why we became mermaids," she said, pointing to the nearby island.

Mako Island loomed above them, mysterious and enticing. Emma cast her memory back to the day she, Cleo and Rikki had been marooned there. It seemed like a lifetime ago – so much had happened since that day. *But we really need to find out what this is all about,* Emma thought. *Cleo's risking everything by doing that job – I have to learn more before something goes really wrong.*

"That's where it happened," she said. "That's where the answers are."

"All right," said Lewis. "Well I'll just pull in my line and then–"

"No, not you, Lewis," said Emma, cutting in and feeling suddenly exhilarated by the

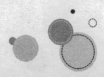

prospect of the swim. "I'm faster on my own."

"Are you really sure that's a good i–"

He was hit in the face with a huge splash of water as Emma turned and darted towards the island.

"–dea?" Lewis finished.

I'm talking to myself, he realized. He looked around at the bobbing boat and sighed. There was no way he was going to return to shore without knowing if Emma was okay. He was in for a long wait.

Lewis started to think about Cleo again. *If she's really going to work at the Marine Park, she'll need all the help she can get*, he thought. *She's surrounded by water at that place. I need to do some serious research and find out more about what water actually does to the girls – and how.* He grinned. *The scientific approach – that's what they need*, he told himself. *And I'm just the guy for the job!*

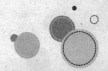

Emma swam through Mako Lagoon, weaving her way through the coral outcrops and swarms of fish. It was magical, and she felt the usual shivers of pleasure and delight up and down her spine. *I don't think I'll ever get used to this!* she thought. *To be able to swim this deep – to see this amazing world – it's like the best present anyone ever had!* She glided downwards, taking her time, entranced by the beauty of the underwater paradise.

It was weeks since she, Emma and Rikki had last been here. After the strange moment in the moon pool, when a blue glow had surrounded them and the water had bubbled and frothed, they had searched for a way out. Emma had discovered a long, underwater tunnel that had led them out into the lagoon. Now she had to find the entrance to the tunnel again – but it was almost impossible to remember where it had been. When they had swum out into the lagoon it had been the middle of the night, and everything had looked different. Emma swam slowly along, peering through the blue-green

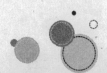

water, hoping to see something she recognized.

Suddenly, she saw two young dolphins swimming towards her. Emma got closer, and they clicked and squeaked as if to welcome her. Emma stopped and smiled at them. *They are so beautiful*, she thought, *so amazing. I wonder if they know what I am?*

One of the dolphins swam up beside her and pressed its fin against her hand. Emma's smile widened – it seemed to want her to hold on. She grasped the fin and held on tight as the dolphin pulled her forwards. The other dolphin swam beside them, plunging delightedly through the water. *Where are they taking me?* Emma wondered. *This is so exciting! I wish that Rikki and Cleo were here with me!*

At last they stopped, and Emma gasped. They were right next to the dark, narrow entrance to the tunnel she had been searching for. *They must have known*, she thought in amazement. *They must have known what I wanted all along!*

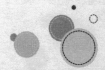

The dolphin stopped and nodded its head at Emma, opening its mouth just as if it were laughing. With a smile of thanks, Emma swam in to the dark cavern.

She slipped along the tunnel, through the strange underwater caverns that she remembered so well. *It's weird*, she thought. *Last time I swam through here, I wasn't a mermaid. It was hard to hold my breath for long enough to get through the tunnel, and I only had legs to swim with!* She cast her mind back to that night. *I hardly knew Rikki at all*, she remembered. *I didn't like her very much at first! And I was so worried about Cleo. Well ... I guess I'm still worried about Cleo ...*

She swam slowly past the barnacle-covered rocks, feeling the fronds of the huge, underwater plants brushing against her body and tail. Excitement was building inside her as she drew near to the magical cave and the moon pool. This was where it had all started. Would she find the answers she was looking for?

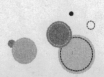

Just before she reached the moon pool, something below caught her eye. Her movement through the water was shifting the sand, and it had uncovered something small and shiny. Emma swam down and reached out her hand to lift it up. She stared in astonishment, her fine blonde hair floating around her face. It was a necklace, with a beautiful silver locket dangling from a fine silver chain. Emma gazed at it for a moment, and then swam on towards the pool. At last she saw the light growing brighter, and finally she surfaced in the circular moon pool.

Emma pulled herself up onto a rocky ledge and looked around. The pool was exactly the same as when she, Rikki and Cleo had found their way in there by accident. A narrow ledge ran around the edge of the cave, but the pool took up most of the space. The water was azure-blue, and it seemed to glow with a soft, flickering light. The high roof of the cave rose up to a round opening at the very top. Sunbeams were shining down, sparkling on the

surface of the pool. It was still so beautiful that it took Emma's breath away for a moment. Everything was quiet and peaceful. It felt as though no one had been in the cave for hundreds of years.

Emma held up the pendant and looked at it thoughtfully. *How long has this been here?* she wondered. It looked very old and it was quite heavy. The sunlight that was streaming through the opening in the roof made the locket gleam. Years of lying in the sand had not spoiled it – the silver was glowing in the strange light that filled the cave. Emma looked around the cave one more time. *I have to go*, she thought. *Lewis will start panicking if I'm not back soon! But I'm sure this necklace is a clue. Whatever mysteries this cave is hiding, we're going to find them out!*

Emma tilted her chin up defiantly and clasped the necklace in the palm of her hand. Then, with a flick of her tail, she had gone.

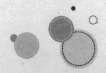

Chapter 3

At the Marine Park, crowds of people had gathered for the dolphin show. The park itself was bustling with activity. There were heart-stopping rides, colourful balloons and lots of amazing aquatic animal enclosures. But the biggest crowd was packed into tiered seats around the dolphin pool, where dolphins were expertly going through their routines.

A handler shot out of the water, lifted from below by a dolphin. She flew into the air and landed on the side of the pool, waving to the audience and laughing. The dolphin was rewarded with fish and squid, and the crowd applauded loudly, cheering and waving.

Part of Cleo's job was to keep the handlers supplied with buckets of fish to feed to the dolphins. Behind the rocky wall of the enclosure, there was a large room where the staff worked. During a performance, Cleo's role

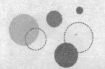
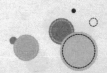

was to race between the enclosure and the back room, filling buckets with fish and squid from a large ice box, and then carrying them out for the handlers.

Cleo was feeling pretty pleased with herself. So far, everything had gone well, thanks to her safety precautions. She was extremely careful as she was handling the fish and squid, and not a single drop of water had landed on her. Just in case she was splashed, the towel that she had tucked into her apron would enable her to stay dry. *Nothing can possibly go wrong*, she told herself, happily.

All eyes were glued to the dolphins. One handler was riding through the water, supported by two dolphins as if he was waterskiing. About halfway up the tiers of seats, a lady was sitting on her own, laughing and clapping in delight. She stood out among the family groups and the young couples, but she didn't seem to notice or care. Her eyes were fixed on the dolphins and gleaming with a look of pride and love, almost as though she was

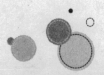

watching old friends.

She was not a young woman, and she was certainly older than 40, but she had a glow about her that made it very hard to decide exactly how old she was. Her hair was blonde, and it hung in two soft coils on either side of her head. She wore loose, flowing clothes in shades of blue and aquamarine, and fish-shaped earrings dangled from her ears.

There was a huge cheer as three dolphins leapt high over a dinghy in the centre of the pool. At the edge of the water, Cleo handed a fresh bucket to another trainer and stepped forward eagerly to watch a few moments of the show. Something about her rapid movement caught the eye of the lady in the audience. The woman's smile disappeared as if someone had wiped it off her face.

Five dolphins leapt into the air simultaneously, and then dived back into the water. The crowd whooped, but the woman was no longer watching the show. She was staring at Cleo in amazement. Without blinking, she rose to her

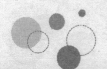

feet to get a better look, moving out of her seat and standing in the central aisle. Everyone else was still cheering and applauding the dolphins – they were paying no attention to this solitary woman. Her eyes were riveted to the dark-haired girl who stood watching the dolphins and smiling.

She stared as Cleo turned and hurried into the back of the enclosure, and then she seemed to reach a decision. As quickly as she could, she hurried down the steps towards the staff area.

In the back room, Cleo was filling another couple of buckets with fish, smiling as she thought about the awesome show that the dolphins were putting on. *They're such gorgeous animals*, she thought, scooping up fish with her tongs and dropping them into a bucket. *I'm so lucky to be working here! I already feel as if I really belong.*

She wasn't thinking about being a mermaid or about having to persuade Emma that she

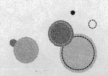

could handle this new job. She wasn't thinking about water or what it could do to her. For the first time that day, she relaxed, and stopped paying attention to what she was doing. Still thinking about the dolphins, she picked up a fish with her tongs, held it over the bucket of water, and let go. *SPLASH*! It hit the water and sparkling drops sprayed through the air. Cleo stumbled backwards, but it was too late. Tiny specks of water splattered over her arms and face.

Cleo grabbed for her towel, but it had fallen into the other bucket and it was sopping wet. She wrung it out, but it was hopeless. *Ten seconds!* thought Cleo in panic. *I've only got ten seconds to get dry or else I'm going to be sprawled on this floor flapping my tail. They'll make me part of the show! Oh help!* She stared wildly around the room, but there were no more towels – and nothing else that she could dry herself on. Panic rose in her as another second ticked past, and then she jumped as someone threw a towel into her arms.

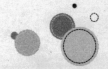

"Try this," said a musical voice.

Cleo looked up and saw a woman smiling at her from the doorway. She looked rather eccentric with her long hair and dramatic clothes, and she wasn't someone Cleo had ever seen before. She was gazing at Cleo with a powerful intensity, but Cleo was too worried about getting dry to notice.

"Timed well, wouldn't you say?" the woman murmured. Her voice was soft and bell-like.

Cleo hastily dried the water drops from her arms and face. Would she be in time? She waited anxiously as ten seconds passed without the appearance of a tail, and then heaved a sigh of relief.

"Er, yeah – thanks," she said, with a nervous smile. "Nearly got salt water in my eye. Would've … stung."

"It *does* sting, doesn't it," said the woman in an eager, understanding voice. "But not when you're actually *underwater*. Why is that, I wonder?"

She opened her bright eyes wide and loo
at Cleo meaningfully. Cleo's mouth fell open
slightly. For the first time she realized that
there was something definitely *odd* about this
lady. It was hard to tell whether she was being
knowing, playful, dotty … or all three. *What
should I do?* thought Cleo, her heart racing.
*What would Emma say? What would Rikki do?
Oh dear! I'm sure they'd know exactly the right
thing to say!*

"I … don't know," she said at last, shaking
her head and wishing that this stranger would
just leave.

"Lots of things are a mystery," the woman
continued with a twinkle in her eye. "Still,
you've got time to learn. Staying *dry*, that's the
big one."

She looked at Cleo expectantly, and Cleo
gaped back at her. The noise of the cheering
crowds and the shouts of the handlers seemed
to fade, as if the sound had been turned down.
The woman's words hung in the air. *Did she just
say what I thought she just said?* Cleo thought,

her head spinning. She could hardly believe what she was hearing! This peculiar woman actually seemed to know that she was a ...

A door behind Cleo suddenly opened.

"Cleo!" said a voice.

Cleo spun around. Miss Geddes was beckoning to her. Feeling numb, Cleo nodded at her. She could hardly piece her thoughts together. *What am I supposed to do now?* she wondered. *Somehow, this woman has found out all about us! I have to warn Cleo and Rikki! No – first I have to ask her how she knows – and what she wants!*

Cleo whirled back around to the doorway, and got another shock. She could see the blue pool through the doorway, and the handlers and dolphins taking their last bows. She could see some of the audience clapping and smiling. But the mysterious lady had completely disappeared.

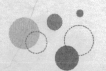

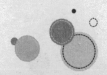

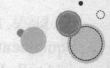

Chapter 4

When Emma finally resurfaced next to Lewis's boat, they hurried back to shore. Emma kept the necklace clasped tightly in her hand as she sped along like a torpedo, and Lewis found it impossible to keep up with her. He thought about the girls as he drove the boat along, wondering what he could do to help them understand what was happening to them. *I just have to carry on with my experiments*, he decided. *I'll get my equipment together and do some more work as soon as I get back.*

By the time Lewis reached the marina, Emma had already returned and dried off. She was leaning against a post at the end of the boardwalk, and as soon as he saw her, Lewis asked her to get Rikki over to her house. *Cleo's still at the Marine Park*, he thought, *but at least I can start on these two!*

Before Emma could say anything about the

necklace, Lewis hurried home to get his equipment. Emma walked towards her house and called Rikki on the way. She didn't know what Lewis was planning, but she wanted her friend's opinion of the necklace – and of Cleo's new job. *I'm sure Rikki will see that Cleo can't work at that place,* she thought. *With Rikki and Lewis to back me up, there's no way Cleo can carry on being so stubborn ... is there?*

Soon, Emma, Lewis and Rikki were sitting on Emma's bed, and Lewis was examining the necklace. The pendant was shaped almost like a tear ... or even a drop of water. A blue precious stone was set into the top of it, and on the back a pattern was embossed into the silver. It looked like three curving lines or waves. Lewis looked at it closely and then turned it over. On the other side was a tiny clasp, which formed the locket. He opened it gently, and saw a small space inside. It was completely empty.

"It looks like a normal necklace to me," he said. *Why would she think I'd know anything*

about jewellery anyway? he asked himself. *I'm a scientist, not a necklace expert!*

He handed the locket back to Emma, who frowned.

"Whatever was in it is long gone," she said, weighing the necklace thoughtfully in her hand. "But I found it at the bottom of the moon pool! It's got to be important."

"Maybe there's some earrings it's supposed to match with," said Rikki with a smirk.

She was sitting on the edge of Emma's bed next to Lewis, and was getting very bored with all this talk about necklaces. She was also slightly annoyed that she had missed out on the trip to Mako Island. Emma had explained that she hadn't exactly planned to go back – it had just happened. *But I would have really liked to be there too*, she thought. Sometimes she felt a little bit left out of things. Cleo, Emma and Lewis had known each other for years. They had been through primary school together and they shared many memories and in-jokes that

27

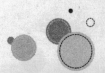

Rikki would never be a part of. Rikki had never quite fitted in anywhere – or wanted to. But since becoming friends with Cleo and Emma, she had found that she had more in common with people like them than she had ever thought.

"I'm just trying to find answers here," Emma snapped, needled by Rikki's tone. *Why does she always have to poke fun at everything?* she wondered in irritation. *Can't she ever be serious?*

"Settle, ladies," said Lewis, who really didn't want to get caught in the crossfire of an argument that involved Rikki Chadwick. "Emma, it still doesn't explain why you guys are mermaids."

"See!" said Rikki in triumph. *Even Lewis agrees with me*, she thought. *That's a first!*

"However," Lewis continued, "I think I've just about figured out which liquids *won't* turn you into fish."

He opened his backpack and pulled out

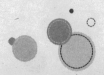

28

several spray bottles, lining them up along the end of Emma's bed. Each bottle contained a liquid of a different colour, and each one was labelled.

If Lewis was hoping to impress them, he had picked the wrong girls. Emma rolled her eyes and examined the necklace again. Rikki scowled at him and looked down at the magazine she had been reading. *I am not a science experiment*, she thought irritably.

Lewis leaned casually forward and picked up the red bottle. He gave Rikki a furtive look. Then his arm moved and he sprayed her arm with the liquid.

"Lewis!" she bellowed. "What are you–? You think you're funny?" She touched the liquid and found that it was slimy and slightly sticky. "Urrgghh!" she cried. "What is that stuff?"

Lewis didn't reply. He had put on his glasses and was looking calmly at his watch, counting down from ten.

"Four, three, two, one …" he paused and looked eagerly at Rikki, who glared back at him, still human. "Hmm. Mostly vegetable oil. No change. Interesting …"

He picked up his notebook and pen, and began to write. Emma hid a smile and Rikki cast him an evil look.

While Lewis was looking through his collection of spray bottles, Emma told Rikki all about Cleo's new job. She ranted about the risks that Cleo was taking and described all the terrible things that she could imagine might happen as a result. Emma shivered when she thought about the dolphin pool. *Standing there all day long,* she thought, *with dolphins splashing and flapping their tails and water flying everywhere! I think she must have gone completely crazy.* However, much to Emma's surprise. Rikki didn't have much to say about it. *Doesn't she see how dangerous it is?* Emma wondered, as Rikki just shrugged and picked up her magazine.

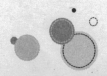

Rikki didn't want to worry about water just then. *It's all we seem to do these days*, she thought. *Right now, I can't be bothered to panic.* She flicked through the articles and pictures, letting her mind go blank.

Emma sat back, passing the necklace slowly from one hand to the other. She was feeling very uneasy. Maybe it was because of Cleo's new job. Maybe it was because she was cancelling her party. Or maybe it was just because Lewis was about to spray her with another mystery liquid …

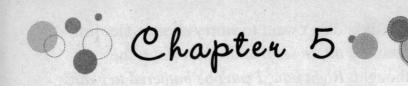

Chapter 5

An hour later, Emma, Rikki and Lewis were still sitting on the bed. More plastic spray bottles were spread around the room, containing liquids of all types and shades. Rikki was painting her toenails bright red, trying to decide what she would do to Lewis if he sprayed her with anything else. Emma was on the phone and Lewis was preparing another batch of liquids.

I don't think it's got anything to do with 'scientific investigations', Rikki thought, darkly. *I think he just likes squirting vegetable oil at me and getting away with it.* She was dividing her attention between her nails and Lewis, who was still playing around with his spray bottles. She wasn't really taking much notice of Emma's conversation at first.

"I really don't think so, Mum," Emma was saying. "Okay? Love you."

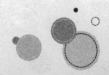

She hung up sadly and Lewis glanced over at her.

"Was that the party again?" he enquired, feeling sorry for her.

He knew how much she had always loved her annual party – she had been holding them every year since anyone could remember.

Emma darted him a *shut up* glare, but it was too late. Rikki's head whipped around, fully alert.

"What party?" she asked.

Lewis winced and shrunk his neck into his shoulders. *How is it I always manage to say the wrong thing?* he wondered.

"Every year, my mum throws this party for me," Emma explained in a resigned tone. "Only this year it's not happening. Can't have heaps of people and drinks spilling and tails appearing ..."

Rikki turned back to her toenails, her lips pursed up. *I haven't been to a party for ages*, she

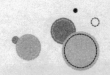

thought. *I need parties! Is Emma saying we can't ever party again, just in case something gets spilled on one of us?*

"When was this party supposed to be?" she demanded.

"Tonight," said Emma, turning the phone over and over in her hands.

"Tonight?" Rikki repeated, raising her eyebrows. "I hope I would've been invited?"

Emma narrowed her eyes, wondering how to get past this without feeling awkward.

"It's not really your scene," she said.

"*Party*?" said Rikki, turning to her in disbelief and waving her nail polish brush in the air. "*Me*? Those words are welded together!"

There was an uncomfortable pause. Emma frowned at Rikki and then looked down at the phone she was still turning over and over in her hands.

"Oh," said Rikki, with a sinking feeling. "You don't want me there – is that it?"

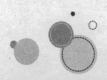

She put on her coolest expression. *What do I care if she doesn't want me there?* Rikki thought furiously. *I guess I'm always going to be on the outside of things, just because I'm the new girl. Sure, we all share this massive secret, and there's no one that I can talk to about it except them. But hey, why should that make them want to include me in their plans?*

Her eyes blazed as she stared at Emma, and her face was hard. Rikki's features were so expressive that they usually revealed her every thought. When she felt hurt, the only way to hide it was to freeze her face into a cold, intimidating mask. She was very good at it. Emma and Cleo had begun to realize that it was a mask, but it was still very uncomfortable to have to deal with.

"Of course I do," said Emma, annoyed that she was being drawn into this discussion. *I wish Rikki wasn't so touchy*, she thought. *And I wish that Lewis would learn when to keep his mouth shut!*

Rikki turned back to her toenails and

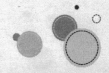

continued slicking nail polish onto them, a little more violently than before.

"So the party's on," said Lewis, who was still scribbling in his notebook. He was trying to work out exactly how much water a liquid could contain without turning the girls into mermaids, and all this talk about the party was way too distracting.

"No!" Emma cried in exasperation. "It's not!"

"Pity," said Rikki in her usual quick-fire style. "Would have been great. Boys ... dancing ... boys."

"It's not really that type of party, Rikki," said Emma with a sigh. *Thanks a lot, Lewis*, she thought. *I know exactly how Rikki's going to react to this – I know she won't get it!*

"What do you mean?" asked Rikki, turning back to Emma again.

What other types of party are there? she asked herself.

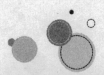

Emma didn't reply, but Lewis grinned as he continued making notes. After a long silence, he decided that it was up to him to reveal the dark truth.

"It's a sleepover," he said, trying to disguise a smile … and failing. *He* knew how Rikki was going to react as well.

Rikki's eyes lit up with glee, and she gazed at Emma in delight. *A sleepover?* she thought. *No way! I thought sleepovers went out with primary school! Oh, this is going to be good!*

Emma looked down, feeling embarrassed and very, very uncool. But before Rikki could decide how to respond, Lewis leaned over and squirted them both with liquid from a green bottle.

"Lewis!" Emma yelled, scrubbing at her leg with a towel.

Rikki wiped her arm distractedly and screwed the top back on her nail polish. She was too busy laughing at Emma to worry about water drops. Lewis had been squirting them

with liquids all afternoon with absolutely no effect, and nothing was going to stop her from well and truly teasing Emma about this!

"So, a sleepover!" she exclaimed in a hugely sarcastic, over-the-top voice. "*Wow*. That is sooo neato."

Emma smiled sourly and slumped back against the headboard. *Come on then, Rikki,* she thought. *Do your worst. Let's get it over with! There's nothing wrong with sleepovers – they're fun!*

"I wish I hadn't painted my nails," said Rikki with a dramatic groan. "We could have painted them *together*! And then we could have had a pillow fight, and plaited each other's hair …"

Lewis tried not to laugh, but he couldn't help it. Then, as he gave a wide grin, there was a blue glow and for a moment Rikki seemed totally transparent. A second later she was a mermaid, her tail dangling off the end of Emma's bed. Her skin shone with a thin layer

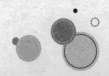

of water, and her blonde hair rippled down her back in long curls.

Emma and Lewis didn't bat an eyelid.

"*That* one had a 32 per cent water content," Lewis informed her, tapping his pen on his chin.

Emma's frown had been replaced by a little smirk.

"You okay?" she asked, opening her eyes wide.

"Fine!" said Rikki through gritted teeth, holding up her hand and flapping her tail. "Thanks, Lewis."

The three of them sat in silence for a moment, staring at the golden tail. Then Lewis started adding to his copious notes.

I'm going to get him for this, thought Rikki. *Just as soon as I get my legs back!*

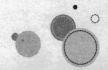

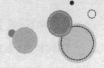

Chapter 6

By the time Rikki had used her power to dry herself and get her legs back, Lewis had collected his bottles and headed home to study his findings … and to stay out of Rikki's way. As Rikki was about to ask Emma a few more teasing questions about her sleepover, Emma's phone rang. It was Cleo, and she sounded as if she was in a terrible state. She said that she had finished work and she wanted them to meet her in the Juice-Net Café immediately. Then she hung up.

Emma fastened the necklace around her neck and told Rikki what Cleo had said. She didn't need to explain any more. Without another word, they raced out of Emma's house and headed for the Juice-Net Café.

As Rikki and Emma hurried across the park towards the café, they wondered what could

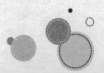

have scared Cleo so badly. *She's been seen,* Emma was thinking. *She got splashed with water in front of a crowd of hundreds of people and she had to jump in with the dolphins.* Her stomach was fluttering. *What if it happened inside one of the Marine Park offices?* she thought suddenly. *That would be even worse! She could have just been lying there, unable to move, with everyone staring ...*

Emma sped up and Rikki had to break into a jog to keep up with her. *Emma needs to chill out,* she thought. *Cleo's always overreacting – I bet it'll be something really minor.* She thought of all the things that could have gone wrong at the Marine Park. *I hope I'm right,* she thought. *Please let me be right!*

They burst into the café and were relieved to see that Cleo wasn't surrounded by scientists or policemen. *That's definitely a good sign,* Emma told herself as they squeezed into the booth where Cleo was waiting. None of them had bothered to order drinks. Emma and Rikki looked at Cleo expectantly.

Cleo had worked herself up into a state of panic, and she was shaking as she told Emma and Rikki all about the strange woman at the Marine Park. She described exactly what she had looked like and what she had said. Emma and Rikki listened in surprise as Cleo stammered out her explanation. Emma looked as worried as Cleo felt, but Rikki screwed up her face doubtfully.

"She 'knows' something?" she repeated, when Cleo had finished. "Like what?"

"I'm not sure," said Cleo with a shrug. "But she knew it was dangerous for me to get water on myself."

"You got *water* on yourself?" exclaimed Emma furiously. "I knew it!"

She was far more worried by this than by some mysterious, eccentric woman who seemed to have vanished into thin air.

"One drop!" said Cleo, astonished by how hysterical Emma was being. *It's usually me who's the drama queen*, she thought. "I wiped it

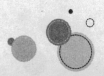

straight off. Nothing happened. I took precautions."

She paused and looked at Rikki and Emma, trying to impress upon them how much thought she had given it. Emma just glared at her, shaking her head in disbelief. Rikki's face was expressionless. She was thinking about Cleo and the whole Marine Park issue. *For once, Cleo is being really brave*, she thought in surprise. *I kind of get where she's coming from on this.*

"I can *do* this job!" Cleo exclaimed, looking around at Rikki, who just rolled her eyes and looked away. She could tell that this was going to turn into a battle of wills between Emma and Cleo.

"And I told you we should have discussed this further," said Emma, her eyes narrowing.

"What would that prove?" asked Cleo. "You're just scared."

Emma sat up straight, hardly able to believe her ears. Cleo had never spoken to her like this

before. *What is going on with her?* she thought.

"No I'm not!" Emma cried, fingering the necklace she had found and feeling suddenly almost shy.

"Yes you are!" said Cleo gently. "Scared for me. *And* too scared to have your own party. Well I'm not living like that any more, Emma. I'm not going to be scared of every drop of water I see."

Good one, Cleo, Rikki thought, and a smile flickered over her face. *She's really starting to get a bit of confidence! First she goes from being scared of water to chasing after illegal fishermen, then she gets a job at the Marine Park, and now she's actually learning to stand up for herself!*

Emma was stumped. She had no idea how to argue with this 'new' Cleo. She looked at Rikki, who shrugged and raised her eyebrows.

"As crazy as it sounds, I agree with Cleo," she said.

Cleo looked at her in delight, and Rikki quickly held up one finger.

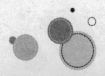

"Just this once," she added with a smile.

Cleo grinned at her and then they both turned back to Emma. She looked down, deep in thought. *Maybe Cleo has a point*, she thought. *I don't want to be scared of every drop of water I see either.* She thought of how Cleo had dared to take this new job, and of how much courage that must have required. *What's the matter with me?* she asked herself. *I have courage too! I'm not going to let this run my life!*

Cleo noticed the necklace glinting in the light.

"Wow," she said. "Where'd you get that?"

"The moon pool at Mako Island," Emma told her.

"It's beautiful," said Cleo.

Emma thought about the moon pool, and how calm and peaceful she had felt in there. The pool was magical and enticing, but it was part of another world. Right now, they had to exist in this one.

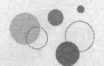

Cleo watched her friend closely, almost holding her breath. She knew that Emma needed to be able to rationalize things, and yet the whole mermaid secret had thrown all her thoughts into chaos. *But I know that she'll see I'm right, in the end*, Cleo thought. *Whatever happens, life can't stand still because we have tails.*

Rikki was watching Emma too, wondering what she was going to do. *I don't think she's got a chance of persuading Cleo to quit her job, and she knows it*, Rikki thought.

Emma bowed her head for a moment, and then brought her chin up as though she had decided something. She flipped open her phone and dialled her home number. After a few rings, she heard her mum's voice.

"Hi Mum," she said, and then she paused and took a deep breath. "I need you to start texting the invitations."

She looked up at her friends and her eyes sparkled. Cleo smiled at her, but Rikki's

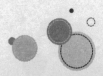

expression went blank again. *I guess I'm on my own tonight then*, she thought.

Meanwhile, Emma's mum was rattling off questions.

"Yes," said Emma, "all the girls on the list ..." she watched Rikki's face, "... plus Rikki."

Rikki couldn't hide her smile as Emma grinned at her and hung up. Even if it was a sleepover party, it still felt good to have been invited.

Cleo looked at Emma in delight. *Emma always has a great time at her party*, she thought. *I am so glad that she has decided to keep up the tradition!*

"Cleo's right," Emma said. "If I don't have this party, it's like I'm not even putting up a fight."

The three friends looked at each other and smiled. It felt as if they were finally taking control of their lives again – and it felt good!

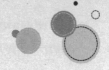

Chapter 7

The girls stayed in the café, and Emma told Cleo about what she had done out at Mako Island that morning. Cleo was delighted when she heard about the dolphins and how they had shown Emma the way back to the cave. Rikki made her laugh by describing Lewis's experiments with water, and after their worries and stresses, they all started to relax and look forward to the party that evening. They had all forgotten about the mystery woman at the Marine Park.

The girls were so focused on their conversation that they didn't notice they were being watched. At a nearby table, Zane Bennett was sitting with Miriam and Tiffany. His eyes kept flicking over to the three girls in the corner. Finally, he leaned over and whispered something to his companions. They giggled and nodded eagerly. Then he stood up

and walked over to the counter, where he ordered something in a low voice.

Zane Bennett was the rudest, most arrogant boy at the girls' school. He acted as if he owned the world, just because his rich, obnoxious father was an important man in the town. Zane was a bully, and he liked making other people feel small, but he seemed to have a special dislike for Rikki, Emma and Cleo.

Miriam was the only person at school more vain and self-important than Zane, and that was saying something. She was spoilt and spiteful, and she liked nothing better than putting other people down. Tiffany wasn't quite as bad, but she was silly enough to think that Miriam was cool.

Emma, Rikki and Cleo had just started to discuss the party when Zane walked over to their table. He put a tray of drinks down on their table and gave them his oiliest smile.

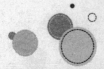

"Three frozen colas," he said.

"What about them?" Rikki asked smoothly.

Zane's smile wavered for a moment. Of all the girls at school, none could get under his skin as quickly and thoroughly as Rikki Chadwick.

Emma stared up at him suspiciously, but Cleo reached out and picked up a drink with a smile. The others were too busy looking at Zane to notice.

"You looked thirsty," said Zane, opening his eyes wide like an innocent child. "Enjoy."

He gave them a smile as if to say that was all the reason he needed. Then he turned and went back to join Miriam and Tiffany at their table.

Emma and Rikki glanced at each other knowingly, but Cleo was thirsty. *Maybe he's just being nice*, she thought, and she took a sip before either of the others could stop her. Then she pulled a disgusted face and put the drink down hurriedly.

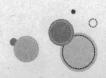

"Prune juice?" asked Emma.

Cleo nodded, and Rikki looked up at the ceiling. *That guy is the biggest idiot on the planet*, she thought. *No, that's not fair. He's the biggest idiot in the whole universe!*

She turned to glare at Zane, who was cracking up with Miriam and Tiffany. Their tinkling giggles irritated Rikki even more.

"Mature, Zane," she said with heavy sarcasm. "Real mature."

Zane just grinned back at her. It felt great to have got under her skin for once.

Just then, a mobile phone beeped with a message nearby. Its owner, Alyssa, read the screen excitedly.

"Emma's sleepover's on!" she squealed to the friend she was sitting opposite.

Miriam turned around to look at her as a second phone beeped with a message across the café.

"Hey, party at Emma's!" exclaimed another girl to her friend in delight. "Did you get one?"

The phone at another table beeped … and another … and another. Girls called out to each other and waved at Emma, promising that they would be there. The usually peaceful vibe of the Juice-Net Café was broken up with the sound of phones beeping and buzzing.

Emma played with the necklace, smiling with Cleo and Rikki at the general excitement. *This feels great*, she thought, looking all the happy, excited faces of her friends. *I'm glad Cleo talked me into it! Now all I have to think about is food … and drinks … and entertainment … oh dear. I think I'm going to need some help!*

Luckily, Cleo was really happy to pitch in and help out. They knew that Emma's mum would have made some snacks, but they also knew how hungry girls could get at a sleepover. Rikki half closed her eyes as Emma and Cleo eagerly discussed practicalities.

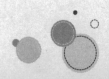

Before long, most of the girls in the café had received text messages – except Miriam and Tiffany. Miriam's expression had turned very sour and Tiffany was tense, waiting for the explosion. She had hung around with Miriam long enough to have reason to dread her temper.

Zane looked down at Miriam's bright pink phone.

"Battery dead?" he enquired with a smirk.

"Oh, as if I'd go to her stupid party anyway," Miriam snarled.

Zane laughed at her embarrassment, and then he was struck by an idea. He didn't have anywhere better to be that evening, and he had really enjoyed the feeling of teasing Emma, Rikki and Cleo. There was one sure-fire way to really wind them up.

"Why don't *we* go?" he said to Miriam, his eyes full of mischief. "You and me."

"Um, I don't think we're invited," said Miriam. "Surprise!"

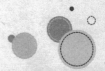

"Aw, come on," wheedled Zane. "Who needs an invitation?"

Miriam looked at him for a moment, thinking it over. Then she gave a smile – and not a very nice one.

That's not such a bad idea after all, she thought. *I'll teach that stuck-up swimming queen what happens when she doesn't invite me to a party!*

They looked over at the three girls, who were deep in conversation. Emma was still playing with her necklace, dangling it between her fingers as she talked. The gleaming silver caught Miriam's eye, and she sat up a little straighter.

I wonder where Emma got that necklace, she thought. *That's a really nice antique. You can't just go out and buy something like that.*

Her eyes narrowed. If there was one thing that Miriam hated, it was anyone possessing something that she couldn't have. It was the necklace that finally decided it. She told Zane

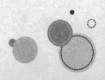

that she would crash the party with him – as long as she had a new outfit to wear.

Zane agreed immediately – if there was one thing he had plenty of, it was money.

He looked over at the three girls again. Emma and Cleo were sitting straight up, eagerly chattering. Rikki was leaning back casually, grinning at them both and injecting an occasional wry comment about the delights of nail painting and hair plaiting. They were having fun, and unexpectedly Zane found himself feeling almost jealous. He scowled and snapped out of it. *Those girls need to be taught a lesson*, he thought. *Tonight, they're going to get a whole lot more than they're bargaining for!*

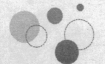

Chapter 8

Later that evening, lights blazed from Emma's house as she and Cleo prepared for the party. Cleo was in charge of drinks and food. She had thought hard about how to keep the danger of spillage to a minimum, and then she had had a brainwave. She finished screwing the lid on a large drink cooler with a tap at the bottom. *That's five bowls of punch and not a drop of liquid in sight*, she thought, feeling very pleased with herself.

She beamed at the four other drink coolers that were ready for action, and then pulled some bags of health snacks out of the cupboard.

Emma was working hard to make the lounge room cosy and sleepover-friendly. She had piled cushions and pillows all over the floor and lit table lamps to give the room a warm glow. She smiled gratefully at Cleo as she dropped some

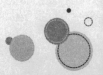

more pillows on the floor. *I'm lucky to have such a great friend*, she thought. *There was hardly any time to get this party ready – I couldn't have done it without her.*

"Em?" Cleo said, wondering how to phrase her question as tactfully as she could. "Are you sure alfalfa and blackcurrant juice is *really* the way you want to go?"

"What do you mean?" asked Emma, frowning slightly. *I always have alfalfa and blackcurrant juice*, she thought. *I like alfalfa and blackcurrant juice. What's wrong with it?*

She moved a faux-fur beanbag into the middle of the room and turned to stare at Cleo.

"Well, I just thought maybe this year, now that you've quit the swimming team, it'd be a good chance to try something new," said Cleo, hopefully.

"Like what?" Emma asked, completely mystified.

Cleo spread her arms wide, searching for the right words. Then she shrugged – it was best

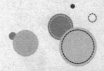

just to be blunt.

"Sugar," she said.

"Oh sure!" gasped Emma, shocked to her core. "And why don't we have full-cream milk while we're at it? That's just crazy-talk."

Cleo let it go – she had known Emma for too long to want to argue with her on healthy eating issues. Emma had dreamed of being an Olympic swimmer since she was old enough to know about the Olympics, and she had always been fanatical about eating healthily and looking after her body. *Old habits die hard*, thought Cleo, with a philosophical shrug. *She's having the party – that's the main thing.*

Emma picked up the drinking bottles that Cleo had been setting out. They were plastic milkshake bottles with an all-in-one lid and straw. They were brightly coloured and fun, and Cleo had thought of them when she was trying to figure out a way to keep liquids out of their way.

"Are you sure people are going to go for

these?" Emma asked, doubtfully.

"Sure," said Cleo breezily, picking one up and looking at it with pride. "People will love them. Individual bottles. Any spillage – contained!"

"And these?" Emma asked, pointing at the various piles of towels that were strategically placed on tables and chairs around the room.

"Just say your mum was doing the washing," said Cleo with a shrug.

Just then, Emma's mum, Lisa, walked in. Her face lit up when she saw what they had been doing.

"The room looks great!" she said, looking around at the inviting piles of bedding, pillows and cushions. "Don't worry, I'm not going to hang around. There's sushi for starters, we've got soy and tofu burgers for mains, and ..." she glanced in puzzlement at the piles of towels, "... you might want to think about putting away these towels?"

"Thanks, Mum," said Emma.

Just then there was a knock at the door – the first guests had arrived. Cleo and Emma looked at each other in excitement.

"I'll make myself scarce," said Lisa with a smile. "Have fun!"

She left, and Emma ran to open the door. There was no going back now.

"Hi!" she said when she saw the group of girls on the doorstep. "Come in! Right on time!"

The girls walked in, laden down with sleeping bags, magazines, makeup and DVDs.

"Hi Emma!" said Caitlin. "Hi Cleo!"

"Hey Emma, how are you doing?" called another friend.

Cleo put a few more beanbags into the centre of the room as the guests came in and made themselves comfortable. *I love sleepovers!* she thought. *Tonight is going to be the best fun ever!*

A little later, the party had really settled in. Caitlin was playing with the stereo, lining up some chilled-out music to create a really laid-back atmosphere. A few girls were already poring over magazines, while Emma was laying out more food on the dining table. Cleo was helping some of the guests to plan their sleeping arrangements. There was a rising murmur of conversation and laughter.

Emma picked up a platter of salad and walked up to her friends Alyssa and Fiona to offer it to them. They grinned at her – they were on the swimming team and it was a long time since they had really spent time with her.

"Your mum's still serving vegetable salad, right?" asked Fiona. "I've brought my dietary supplement just in case."

Emma smiled – these girls thought exactly the same way she did.

"I may not be on the swimming team any more, but I still eat sensibly," she said with a laugh.

She felt a sudden twinge of pain that she knew was not physical. It was a pain in her heart. She really missed being on the swimming team. She missed the discipline of training; she missed the company of friends who felt the same way she did about swimming; most of all she missed the feeling that she was working towards her greatest ambition.

I just have to forget about that, she told herself, sternly. *It's not like I never swim!* She pulled herself back into the present and realized that Fiona and Alyssa had been speaking.

"... and I'm tapering," Alyssa was saying, "but I've got to be up at five in the morning for training. So's Jay – so's Kelly."

"Relax," said Emma. "I've set up a quiet room upstairs for anyone who has to crash early."

"That's our Emma," said Alyssa. "We so miss you on the swimming team."

"Thanks," said Emma. "I still swim –

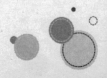

occasionally."

Alyssa and Fiona looked at her sympathetically, obviously thinking that she hardly spent any time in the water any more. Emma repressed a smile. *If only they knew!* she said to herself, thinking of the countless expeditions that she, Rikki and Cleo had taken underwater.

They had played hide and seek with dolphins among coral reefs. They had swum faster than speeding torpedoes and discovered deep-sea paradises that even experienced divers had never seen. *I have definitely got nothing to complain about!* thought Emma.

"These are so cute!" said Fiona, holding up one of the drinking bottles that Cleo had suggested. Cleo heard her and smiled at Emma.

It's all working out, she thought, happily.

Chapter 9

When they had sorted out where they were going to sleep, Cleo suggested that they all give each other a makeover. The idea was greeted with squeals of delight and everyone grabbed a beanbag and pulled out their makeup bags. They settled down to some serious pampering, painting their nails, testing out new colours on each other and exchanging makeup tips and tricks.

As they were all putting the finishing touches to the new looks they had created for each other, there was a sharp rap at the door. Cleo slicked some clear gloss onto Alyssa's lips while Emma went to answer the door. Rikki was standing there, wearing her widest grin. Emma smiled and stepped back to let her in. Rikki strolled in and stopped short when she saw the group of giggling girls and the mass makeover. He grin faded and her expression

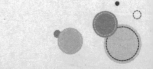

changed to one of horrified disbelief. She folded her arms and stared.

"That's *amazing*," one girl was saying to her friend as she pointed out a colour in an eyeshadow palette.

"Oh, that's really *nice*," squealed another as she looked in the mirror at her new style.

"I told you it wasn't your scene," said Emma, unable to hide a little smile at Rikki's reaction.

"I can't believe it's *anyone's* scene," said Rikki in genuine shock.

Fingering her silver locket, Emma looked at all her friends, seeing them through Rikki's eyes for a moment. *It might not be the edgiest party ever,* she thought. *But I really like all these people, and everyone's having fun. That makes it the coolest party in the world!* At that moment there was a ring on the doorbell.

Emma had left the front door open after letting Rikki in, and she had left the way clear for two people who were not welcome at all.

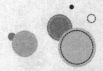

Without waiting to be asked, Miriam walked in, closely followed by Zane.

Miriam was dressed in a hideous and extremely expensive new pink top. Her hair was scraped back from her forehead, giving her an even colder, harder look than usual. Miriam was a pretty girl, but she spoiled it with her scowls, her insults and her attitude. Zane was carrying two trays of delicious-looking food. Miriam looked at Emma and folded her arms.

"I don't know which of my numbers you sent my invitation to," she said with a sneer. "But it managed to get lost."

"So how about joining it?" said Rikki, eyeballing Miriam. *Of all the arrogant, stuck-up, interfering snobs!* she thought.

Miriam just rolled her eyes and walked past them into the lounge room. At that moment, Emma's mum walked downstairs.

"Zane!" exclaimed Lisa. "Fancy seeing you here!"

Emma glanced at Rikki, who looked as if

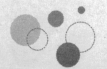

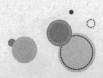

she was about to say something awful, and gave her a warning look. *I really don't want this to turn nasty*, she thought.

"Glad you could make it," she said aloud, with a tight smile.

"Come in!" Lisa told Zane, leading him through to the kitchen. "What a delightful surprise!"

Miriam had walked through the lounge room, sneered at the other guests and was now standing in the kitchen, wearing a bored expression.

"And Miriam!" Lisa continued, moving over to hug her. "I haven't seen you in ages."

Miriam put on a sweet, friendly expression and hugged Lisa back as if she were her best friend.

"Yes, it's been a while!" she said.

Rikki and Emma stared in disgust from the hallway.

"I can't stand gatecrashers," said Rikki

through gritted teeth. "You want me to kick them out? Just say the word."

Emma was tempted for a moment, but then she shook her head.

"Forget it," she said. "I don't want to make a scene in front of my mum."

She shot Rikki a half smile and headed towards the kitchen. Rikki followed her, frowning. *I don't get it*, she thought. *I would just throw them both out right now. But I guess it's not my sleepover!*

Emma and Rikki walked into the kitchen just in time to hear Lisa say, "And what about you, Zane?"

Zane turned to Emma. His face and his voice were casual and friendly, but his eyes were mocking and challenging her.

"Your mum has invited us to stay and eat with you guys," he said in his nicest voice.

He's spectacularly good at putting on an act

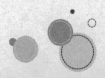

in front of parents, thought Rikki. *What a slime!*

Emma pursed up her lips. Rikki paced behind her like an angry leopard. There was a long, tense silence as they all stared at each other.

"I hope there's enough food," Emma said at last.

"Oh, well Zane must have thought the same thing," smiled Lisa, who didn't seem to have noticed the sudden bad atmosphere. "He's brought along a contribution."

Zane lifted up one of the trays he had carried in. It was full of tiny puff pastries.

"Pastries," he said. "Gluten-free."

"Oh, very thoughtful!" exclaimed Lisa.

That is the last straw, thought Emma.

"Mum," she said, raising her eyebrows and smiling as sweetly as she could. "Can I talk to you?"

Emma took Lisa by the hand and pulled her out into the hallway.

"Mum, they weren't invited," she said in a low voice.

She watched Zane pick up a plate of sushi and feed a piece to Miriam. He looked around the room, checking out the girls, and then Miriam reached up and moved his face so that it was looking at her again.

"Oh well, they're here now," said Lisa, who couldn't see what the problem was.

"And you asked them to stay!" Emma exclaimed.

"Emma, you and Zane may not get on the way you used to, but he's an old family friend. You should make more of an effort."

As Lisa glanced over at Zane, he made a great show of enjoying her sushi. He waved and smiled.

"He's a lovely young man," Lisa added, as Emma rolled her eyes. "All right, time for me to go. Have a good one."

She left and Emma's shoulders slumped.

There's nothing I can do, she thought.

Cleo and all her guests were sitting on the cushions and beanbags, chattering. They had wrapped themselves up in blankets.

"Hey, let's get into our PJs!" suggested Alyssa suddenly.

"Yeah!" cried several of the other girls.

They all jumped up and started to locate their sleepover bags.

Zane stared around at the giggling guests as they hurried upstairs to get changed. He couldn't believe his luck. He was the only boy at a party full of girls! Miriam moved his face back to look at her again and fixed him with a glare.

Rikki was still standing in the kitchen. She leaned on the counter, staring at the girls as they giggled, gossiped and changed into their pyjamas. Rikki shook her head slowly.

"It's *got* to be a parallel universe," she said to herself.

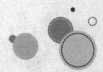

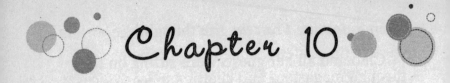
Things just got steadily worse as the evening went on.

When the guests had changed into their pyjamas, Zane suddenly became the life and soul of the party. He could turn on the charm when he wanted to, and at that moment he was charm itself – telling jokes, giving compliments and showering everyone with attention. Soon he was surrounded by almost all the girls, who giggled and flirted as he chatted to them. Most of the girls on the swimming team didn't know Zane, and they didn't realize how two-faced he really was.

"So what now?" he asked them in a soft, smooth voice. "I'm bored."

Miriam was standing next to him, her arms folded. She didn't look as though she was enjoying the party very much at all. Her expression was thunderous, but Zane didn't

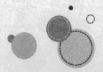

seem to notice. The few girls who did know him were sitting quietly on beanbags, flicking through magazines and chatting in low voices.

Emma, Rikki and Cleo were sitting around the dining table. They were still dressed, and they were very, very annoyed.

"Well, this is boring," said Cleo flatly. "Everyone's just talking to Zane."

"He's up to something," said Rikki, her voice heavy with suspicion and foreboding.

"Yeah," Emma snapped. "Taking over my party."

As all her guests went into another fit of giggles, her frown deepened. *I've had enough of this*, she thought.

"Zane, I need to speak to you," she said. "*Now*."

"Sorry, Emma," Zane said with a chuckle. "Can't. The girls need me."

The girls giggled again.

"Zane–" said Emma, getting to her feet.

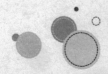

"Emma, really," he grinned, enjoying the tease. "I'd be letting them down."

She marched over to the huddle of girls, pushed them aside and grabbed Zane by the arm.

"They'll cope," she told him.

"Excuse me, ladies," said Zane as he was dragged away. "I think I'm needed for a moment – in *private*."

They sighed and then giggled again. Emma scowled and pulled Zane out of the room.

Rikki watched them go, and then turned her attention back to the girls, who were waiting eagerly for him to come back. *They must be mad*, she thought. *The fumes from all that makeup have gone to their heads. It's the only explanation!*

Suddenly, something in the kitchen caught her eye. It was the tray of pastries that Zane had brought with him. Rikki's thoughts whirled

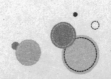

and she remembered the prune juice incident earlier that day. *He's definitely up to something,* she thought, *and I think I know what it is!*

Upstairs, Emma walked into her room, turned, folded her arms and glared at Zane. She didn't like him being in her bedroom, but it was the only place she could speak to him alone. She waited in silence, hoping that he would offer an apology.

However, Zane just swaggered across her room to stare at the wall where her photos and swimming trophies were displayed. Her shelves were crammed with bronze, silver and gold trophies, shiny medals and framed certificates. There were photos of her winning races and accepting prizes, as well as pictures of her swimming idols. She might not be able to swim in competitions any more, but that didn't mean she couldn't have all her memories on display.

Suddenly a smile flashed across Zane's face. He reached out and picked one of the

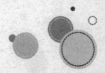

photographs up.

"Ahh, check this – our old primary school photo!" he exclaimed.

Zane stared down at the picture. Back then, he and Emma had been friends. In the photo, he was standing behind her, grinning. Emma had her hair in two neat blonde plaits. Emma frowned. *This is no time for a trip down memory lane*, she thought.

"Whatever you're trying to pull, Zane, forget it," Emma snapped.

"Hey, I'm just here with Miriam," said Zane.

"Oh really?" said Emma. "And what does your 'girlfriend' think of you flirting with everyone else?"

"*Girlfriend*?" Zane repeated in astonishment. "I don't think so. Miriam's the girl I let follow me around whenever it suits me."

For a moment he slipped out of the act he had put on all evening.

"You are such a user!" said Emma, surprised

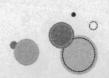

to find herself feeling sorry for Miriam.

"Me?" Zane exclaimed. "Hey, I bought her a new outfit for tonight. She's getting a good deal."

He smirked at her frustration and put the photo back on her shelf. At that moment, Rikki appeared in the doorway. She was carrying one of the trays of pastries that Zane had brought.

"Pastries, anyone?" she asked.

She walked up to Zane and held out the tray, challenging him.

"I really shouldn't," said Zane quickly. "They're a gift. For you and your guests."

Emma caught on straight away. Rikki suspected that Zane had done something to the pastries, just like he had tried to trick them with the prune juice.

He's not getting away with that trick a second time, she thought angrily.

"But you *are* a guest, Zane," she said, smiling sweetly. "Go on – go ahead."

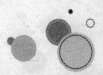

Zane hesitated, and then reached for one of the pastries. But Rikki wasn't about to let him pick the one he wanted. *He might have made sure that one was okay*, she thought.

"How about … *that* one?" she said, pointing.

Emma grinned as Zane's face fell and he looked at Rikki nervously.

Then he picked up the pastry, popped it in his mouth and ate it.

"Mmm, delicious," he said, enjoying their shocked expressions. "Perhaps I'll eat them all myself."

He looked from Rikki to Emma, who were now seething.

"What?" he asked, faking a look of hurt surprise. "You didn't think I'd be so immature as to put prunes or something in them, did you?"

Emma and Rikki exchanged infuriated glances. Zane smirked – his trick had worked.

"Okay," said Emma, who had just officially

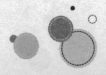

lost her temper. "Let's go, Zane."

She shoved him out of her bedroom. Rikki followed, her expression stony.

"You'll be sorry," said Zane, chuckling. "You're looking at the life of the party here, girls."

He half stumbled as Emma pushed him firmly down the stairs and towards the front door.

As they passed the kitchen, Emma's guests spotted her and started calling out her name.

"Hey Emma!" called Alyssa. "Come and show us your necklace!"

She had spotted it earlier and wanted to have a closer look – everyone was commenting on it.

"Just a minute," said Emma, turning to Rikki and lowering her voice. "Get rid of him. And do me a favour; keep an eye out. I wouldn't be surprised if he made a reappearance."

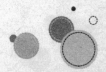

Rikki nodded and turned to Zane as Emma walked back to her party. Without a single word, she pushed him out through the door, waving sarcastically as she did so. As soon as he was outside, she slammed the door shut.

Good riddance, she thought.

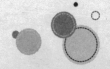

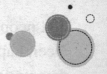

Chapter 11

Emma walked back into the kitchen, smiling at her friends. After the confrontation with Zane, she was getting warm, so she pulled off her blue shirt top and laid it down on the counter. Alyssa and a couple of others gathered around, keen to get a closer look at her new necklace. Emma undid the clasp and held it out towards Fiona, who took it. The silver locket gleamed in the electric light. Nearby, Miriam was watching carefully.

"It's beautiful," said Alyssa.

"It's so pretty," added Fiona, holding it in her hand and admiring it.

Emma smiled. *If only they knew where it came from!* she thought, imagining their faces if they could see her as a mermaid. *They would totally flip out!*

Sometimes she wished that she was able to

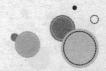
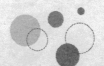

tell people about the wonderful things that had been happening to them. Emma didn't like keeping secrets. But she knew that if the truth ever came out, they would have no peace.

"Are you going to come and get into your PJs?" asked Alyssa, beaming at Emma.

"Yes," said Emma. "I'm just going to go and get some more pillows."

She hurried back upstairs and Fiona put the necklace down over her shirt top on the kitchen counter. A few more girls gathered around to look at it, but then there was a shriek from the other side of the room.

"Towel fight!"

All the girls grabbed towels from the piles that Cleo had left out earlier and plunged into the fray, screaming and giggling. Only Miriam stayed still, close to where the silver necklace lay shining on the counter.

Meanwhile, Rikki was prowling around outside

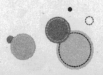

the house, making sure that Zane didn't try to sneak back in. *I can't believe the nerve of the guy,* she thought. *Him and that stuck-up Miriam. Whoever heard of anyone gatecrashing a sleepover, anyway?* she thought she saw a shadow move on the lawn and glared fiercely at it. *After all the trouble it took to persuade Emma to have this party, I'm not going to let Zane spoil it for her,* Rikki thought. *Even if it is a parallel universe ...*

Emma dashed into her room and pulled the pillows off her bed. She turned to leave, but then the trophies and pictures on her wall caught her eye. Emma walked over to them, reaching out to touch the medals that dangled from the packed shelves. *It's weird,* she thought. *Not so long ago, swimming was my whole life. And now, I do miss it ... but this is way more exciting.* She gave a slow, dreamy smile as she rubbed her thumb over the golden surface. It had only been a few weeks since she had become a mermaid and her world had been

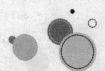

turned upside down. But already, the days when she had been consumed with thoughts of swimming competitions and championships seemed like a lifetime ago. She looked at her pictures of famous swimming champions and her head whirled. *I can swim faster, deeper and further than any of them*, she realized. *Rikki, Cleo and I are probably the fastest swimmers in the world.* She laughed ruefully. *And we can't tell a single person about it!*

Downstairs, Miriam was edging closer and closer to Emma's necklace, keeping one eye on the towel fight, which was ranging all over the lounge room. Her hand twitched, and then Alyssa broke off from the fight and walked into the kitchen, panting and laughing. Miriam froze, still staring at the necklace, and then moved away.

Cleo wasn't joining in with the towel fight; she didn't really like them and they made her

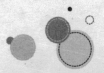

nervous. Instead, she was curled up on one of the beanbags, flicking through a magazine. She winced as the edge of a towel flicked her arm.

I wish Emma would hurry up and come downstairs, she thought. *I'd much rather settle down and start watching a film than get flicked with towels!*

Alyssa went to pour herself another drink from the cooler tap, but there was only a dribble left. She picked up the cooler and opened the lid. From the other side of the room, Cleo saw her opening the container and went into red alert. She dropped the magazine, scrambled to her feet and hurried over.

"What's the problem?" Cleo asked.

"It's just about empty," Alyssa explained.

"I'll fix it," said Cleo.

She tried to take the cooler container, but Alyssa hung on to it.

"It's okay," she said. "I can do it."

"No, no, no," Cleo insisted, pulling at the

container. "You're a guest."

"No, really, it's fine," Alyssa told her.

It was developing into a tug of war. Why doesn't she just let go? Cleo thought. I wish she would just let me deal with this! The cooler tipped from side to side as they pulled at it, and the last dregs of the drink were sloshing around inside. Then, as they struggled, Alyssa hand knocked into the tap that released the drink. To Cleo's horror, the last drops of liquid tipped all over her hand.

"I am so sorry," gasped Alyssa.

Cloe hardly heard her. She froze, but her eyes darted around the room, searching for the nearest pile of towels. But the other girls were still racing around, flicking each other with them. There wasn't a single towel in reach, and if she tried to take one off another of the girls, they would just think it was part of the game and start a tug of war. Alyssa was using the kitchen towel to wipe up the spilled drink from the counter.

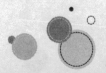

Everything seemed to go into slow motion. Desperately, Cleo looked around the crowded room. She had fewer than ten seconds before she turned into a mermaid. There was no way that she was going to get through the gauntlet of girls in time. *I can't dry myself and I can't get out of this room!* she thought in a panic. *Where are Rikki and Emma? I'm trapped!*

Alyssa was staring at Cleo. *It was only a bit of juice*, she thought in surprise. *She looks as if she's gone mad! What's the matter with her?*

Alyssa opened her mouth to say something, but at that moment, Cleo noticed the only door that she had any chance of reaching. Barging past the few girls who were in her way, she charged across the room, flung open the door and dived in, pulling the door shut behind her. It was the closet.

Inside, she found herself pressed up against a vacuum cleaner and trampling on shoes. Her heart hammered against her chest as she heard the cries of surprise and curiosity outside. Then

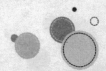

she felt something soft beside her. She reached out and gave a sigh of relief. It was a sleeping bag!

The other girls stopped their towel fight and stared at the closed closet door. They exchanged surprised looks and then stared at the closet door again. What was Cleo doing?

"Why did she go in there?" said one girl, uncertainly.

"Are you okay in there?" asked Fiona, trying to peer through the slatted door.

"Hang on!" Cleo yelled, pressing herself back as she saw Fiona's face through the slats.

Everyone gathered around the closet door, puzzled and amused.

"Hey, Cleo?" said Alyssa. "The party's out here."

"Just a second!" called Cleo. "I'll be out in a minute!"

Fiona turned to look at the others, and they exchanged questioning looks. There was

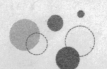
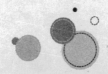

definitely something weird going on.

"Cleo?" said Fiona, tugging at the closet door.

Something seemed to be holding the door on the other side. Fiona pulled harder and then the door shot open. Cleo was standing in the closet, wobbling slightly. She was completely encased in a sleeping bag. It was tied up tightly around her neck and the hood was over her head. She swayed unsteadily for a moment and tried to look casual. But there was no way that her tail would allow her to stay upright. She fell forward and landed face first in a beanbag.

The other girls burst into laughter as Cleo looked up at them and smiled brightly, as if everything was completely normal. Her mind was racing as she tried to think of a reason why she might have just jumped into the closet.

"About time we got comfy and hit the DVDs, right girls?" she said eventually.

Her arms were pressed down by her sides and she could only wriggle from side to side like a snake, but at least she was hidden.

"Yeah!" chorused the other girls, reaching for their sleeping bags and pillows.

A mischievous light came into Alyssa's eyes as she looked down at Cleo's sleeping-bag cocoon.

"Hey, I've got an idea!" she said.

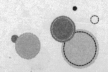

Chapter 12

Alyssa's idea was simple – sleeping-bag bumps! They wrapped a willing guest up in a sleeping bag, making sure that the hood was pulled nice and tight. Then they gathered around her and lifted her high into the air, bouncing her up and down until she was screaming as if it was a fairground ride. The girls shrieked with laughter as they lifted her higher and higher.

Cleo watched from the safety of her sleeping bag. She felt very pleased with her quick reactions. *I'll just stay in here until I dry off*, she thought. *It's really hot in here so it won't take too long. It was lucky I saw that closet – and even luckier that there was a sleeping bag inside!* She smiled and felt her heart rate return to normal. *That was really scary for a minute!* she thought.

But Miriam noticed Cleo's smile and saw the chance for some mischief.

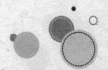

"Now, this was *Cleo's* idea," she said. "I think we should give her a turn."

"Yes, Cleo," said one of the other girls. "Now it's your turn!"

Cleo gulped and closed her eyes in horror for a moment. *One touch and they'll know those aren't legs in there*, she thought. *Oh, why did Miriam have to be here? She's only doing it because she knows I hate this sort of thing!*

She sank further down into the sleeping bag. But the other girls were cheering in agreement and turning towards her.

"Cleo! Cleo!" they chanted. "*Cleo! Cleo!*"

"You're risking serious injury!" said Cleo desperately. "I'm heavier than I look!"

"*Cleo! Cleo!*"

All the girls were facing her and chanting … all except one.

Miriam hadn't just set the others on Cleo to be mean – she had a plan. While the other girls

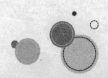

were busy moving in on Cleo, she edged her way slowly towards Emma's necklace, which was still lying on the kitchen counter.

"*Cleo! Cleo!*" the girls laughed behind her.

"Oh come on," Cleo begged, racking her brains for something that would stop them. "I suffer from motion sickness. And air sickness."

"*Cleo! Cleo!*" they went on, drawing closer and closer around her.

In the kitchen, Miriam looked down at the silver locket, with its precious stone glinting in the light.

That's much too nice for Emma Gilbert to be wearing, she thought. *And it would go so well with my new top!*

"Cleo! Cleo!"

The girls were pressed around Cleo now, reaching out their arms to touch her and lift her up.

Where is Emma all this time? Cleo thought in despair. *Where has Rikki wandered off to?*

Where are my friends when I need them?

Miriam reached out her hand to take the necklace.

"*Cleo! Cleo!*"

There's only one thing for it! Cleo thought, with a certain burst of clarity. *I'll have to risk using my power!* She wriggled her hand free of the sleeping bag as fast as she could.

Cleo could make water move however she wanted, but she hadn't yet mastered the subtle control that she would have liked. With her hand stiff and pointing towards the kitchen, she twisted it half a turn. She focused on the drinks bottles and coolers. Trying to ignore the chanting girls around her, she forced all her fear and strength through her fingertips and out towards the containers. They started to vibrate and swell. There was a deep, bubbling sound and then – *POP*! With an almighty bang, all the drinks coolers exploded. Each drink bottle erupted like a mini geyser. Fountains of red,

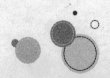

94

staining liquid spurted high into the air ... and drenched Miriam from head to foot.

The girls screamed and leapt up, forgetting all about Cleo and the sleeping-bag bumps. They gathered around Miriam, staring in wonder at the kitchen. Everything in and around it was sopping wet. Juice ran down the walls, dropped from the ceiling and puddled on the floor.

"Eurrghh!" screamed Miriam, as she wiped alfalfa and blackcurrant juice out of her eyes. Her perfect mascara was running down her face, making her look like a panda. She shook herself like a wet dog, and Cleo buried herself deeper in her sleeping bag. *Thank goodness she doesn't know it was me!* she thought.

While the others were picking up towels and trying to dab Miriam dry, Cleo took her opportunity to escape. Wriggling like a contortionist, she pulled her other arm out of the sleeping bag and then dragged herself out

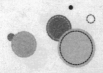

of the lounge room, around the corner and into the hallway. She could hear the others' amazed voices and Miriam's furious squeals of rage. Puffing and panting, she slid across the hall, up the stairs and made it into the bathroom without anyone seeing her. Almost crying with relief, she locked the door and untangled herself from the sleeping bag. I'm safe, she told herself. Not even Miriam can get through a locked door! She picked up the hairdryer, cranked up the settings to the hottest possible temperature and began to dry her scaly tail.

At that moment, Emma walked in to the kitchen carrying two pillows. She stopped, staring in astonishment at the dripping ceiling and wet floor. The other girls were hovering uncertainly, still staring with open mouths. They were scared to get too close to the drinks containers in case they exploded again. Emma realized that Cleo must have had something to do with this. She thought fast and quickly plastered a smile on her face.

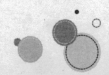

"Not *again*!" she said with a casual laugh. "Every time this room gets hot and full of people, something just ... happens ... to the ... er ... air pressure, and *bang*! There go the drinks!"

"Well those drinks just *ruined* my new *top*!" seethed Miriam.

Emma gave her a weak smile, wondering how she was going to explain the mess to her mum. Then, as she looked around the room at all the confused faces, she realized that Cleo's face wasn't among them. She had completely disappeared. Emma turned and raced out of the kitchen. Something was definitely wrong.

Rikki had just walked in when Emma dashed past her, looking worried. Rikki could hear the murmur of the guests and Miriam's loud complaints. *Hmm, I'd guess there's something going on that doesn't usually happen at sleepovers*, she thought with a smile. She stayed where she was. *If anyone needs me, they can*

come and get me, she thought. *I'm going to stay here and guard the front door. Zane Bennett is not coming anywhere near this party again!*

As Emma hunted through the house, Cleo was patiently moving the hairdryer down her tail. *This is nowhere near as fast as Rikki!* she thought. Rikki's power enabled her to boil water, and in emergencies she could dry off their tails at super-speed by evaporating the water with a quick clench of her hand.

Cleo's heart was still thumping crazily. Her tail seemed to be taking up the whole room, and even though the door was locked, she felt incredibly vulnerable. Then there was a knock on the door. Cleo turned off the hairdryer and froze.

"Cleo, it's me," came Emma's voice. "Open up."

Cleo carefully opened the door and Emma slipped into the room, carrying more towels. She peered out into the corridor to check that

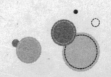

no one was following her, and then locked the door and looked down at her friend.

Cleo looked utterly miserable. Her skin and scales gleamed golden, and her dark hair flowed down her back in thick curls. Emma gave her a comforting smile. *Why is it always Cleo who manages to get herself into these situations?* she wondered.

Cleo switched on the hairdryer again as Emma kneeled down and started to rub her tail with the towels. Not a word was spoken – that had been way too close for comfort.

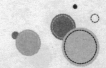

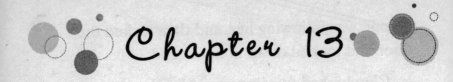

Chapter 13

In the lounge room, Miriam was still scrubbing at her top with a towel, trying to remove some of the red stains. Her makeup was ruined, her hair looked like rats' tails and her expression was absolutely thunderous. She had never had such a rotten evening. First her date had flirted with all the other girls, and then he had been kicked out. Now exploding drinks had damaged her outfit beyond repair.

"You know, I'm thinking this is the worst party I've ever been to," she spat at the other girls. "Thanks for three hours of my life I'll never get back."

No one replied. The other guests had settled down onto the cushions and beanbags again, not sure what to do next. For the first time all evening, Miriam really was the centre of attention ... just not in the way that she would have chosen. The girls stared at her in silence

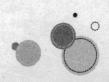

and a few of them giggled. Not one of them seemed to want to stop her from leaving.

Infuriated, Miriam turned on her heel and dropped the stained towel on top of the kitchen counter. Then, so swiftly that it was almost like a magic trick, she picked up Emma's necklace and concealed it in her hand.

Only one person saw what she had done.

Unfortunately for Miriam, that person was Rikki Chadwick ...

Miriam strolled casually around the corner to the front door, and then stopped dead in her tracks. Rikki was standing at the foot of the stairs, leaning against the banister with her arms folded. Miriam stared at her, self-satisfied and impudent.

I can't stand girls like you, Rikki was thinking. Her blue eyes were as hard and sparkling as diamonds. *You're cruel and spiteful and spoilt. You think that everyone ought to do exactly what you say, but you're not going to get*

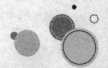

your own way this time!

"Give it back," she said. Her voice was quiet, but there was an air of command in it.

"Give what back?" said Miriam.

"You know what I'm talking about," Rikki said, staring her straight in the eye.

"Get out of my way," said Miriam, dropping her eyes and pushing past Rikki.

Rikki grabbed her arm and Miriam spun around. In the tussle she lost her grip on the necklace and it fell to the floor with a clatter and a thud. Rikki picked it up and then she stared at Miriam again, her eyes demanding an apology. She walked around her in a slow circle, so that Miriam had to keep turning to see what she was going to do.

Miriam was a bully, but unlike most bullies, she wasn't a coward underneath. When her temper was roused, she could lash out like a scorpion. She was used to having her own way, and was prepared to fight tooth and nail to get it. However, she had met her match in Rikki,

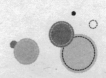

and she knew it.

"I've got better things to do with my time," said Miriam. "Ciao."

She turned towards the door and Rikki gazed in dislike and disgust at her stained back.

"Thief," Rikki stated in a cold, calm voice.

Miriam stopped, paused for a moment and then turned, folding her arms. She looked Rikki up and down. *Who do you think you are?* she thought. *As if I can be threatened by a stupid, badly dressed, unrefined little weirdo nobody like you!* A cruel, vicious smile spread over her face.

"Get over it," she said. "It's your word against mine, and no one's going to believe *you*."

Rikki swallowed hard. She was brave and she wasn't afraid of confrontation, but she didn't know how to react to this kind of attack. She was the new girl in town – she had only been there a few months – and lots of people still didn't know her at all.

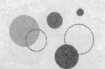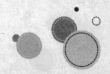

"Hey," Miriam continued, pleased by Rikki's silence. "Some people might even think that *you* took it."

She paused to let this sink in, tipping her head on one side as if she was waiting for a reaction. Rikki said nothing. *I'm not giving her the satisfaction*, she thought, biting her lip.

"See ya!" said Miriam in a cheerful tone.

She smiled and took her time leaving – acting as if she owned the place. Rikki glared at her back, but as soon as the door closed behind Miriam, the defiant light left her eyes.

She's right, she thought, staring down at the floor and clasping the necklace tightly. *Those girls in there don't know me.* Painful thoughts danced in her head. *Why should they believe a word I say?*

In the bathroom, Cleo and Emma worked hard to dry Cleo's tail. At long last there was a blue shimmer and Cleo seemed to turn transparent. A second later, she was back to normal, with

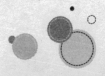

her hair in a long plait and her legs stretched out in front of her. The bathroom floor was hardly visible under the scattered towels and the long sleeping bag. Cleo turned off the hairdryer and put it down. Emma gave her a hand and pulled her up. That was a close one, thought Emma. Cleo sat down on the edge of the bath and Emma sank down beside her, sitting close together and feeling comforted by each other's closeness. They both knew that they had been extremely lucky.

Cleo explained to Emma exactly what had happened while she had been upstairs. Emma couldn't help but laugh when she thought of Cleo struggling with the sleeping bag in the closet. She was starting to feel more relaxed about the danger that water posed to them. *After all*, she thought, *Cleo couldn't have come closer to being found out, and she handled it really well.*

Cleo, however, was feeling very silly and guilty. *I guess I can't do anything right*, she thought. *It was me who got thrown into*

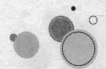

Miriam's swimming pool that time, and it was me who got caught in that fishing net. Now I've almost ruined everything in front of all Emma's friends.

Emma looked closely at her friend. She knew Cleo so well that she could sometimes almost read her thoughts.

"It's not your fault you got wet," Emma said, gently.

"No," said Cleo. "But it's my fault you had the party. I was the one who talked you into it."

"I'm glad you did," Emma told her, with a wide smile. "Otherwise, I'd be stuck in my room watching TV all night."

"At least you'd be safe from blackcurrant and alfalfa juice," said Cleo, laughing a little.

Emma laughed too, and looked down at her hands in her lap. Her expression grew serious as she thought about all the things that had happened that day. She was beginning to understand that they couldn't live their lives risk-free. *We have a massive secret*, she thought,

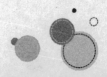

and we can't just hide away from our lives forever. She looked over at Cleo, who was slumped dejectedly next to her. *Cleo has been amazing*, she thought. *Sometimes I think that she's the strongest of the three of us.*

"Cleo, you were right to get the job at the Marine Park," she said. "We can't spend our lives hiding."

"*I* was right?" said Cleo, hardly able to believe her ears. "*Me?*"

Emma nodded, and Cleo's eyes gleamed. She sat up a little straighter.

"Gee, I'll have to get used to that one," she said, nudging Emma's shoulder gently.

They both laughed, and Cleo felt a huge wave of excitement rush through her. *I was so worried about how Rikki and Emma would react to my new job*, she thought. *But they've both been awesome. I have the greatest friends!*

Just then they heard some music start up from the direction of the lounge room – it sounded as though the party was getting started

again. Emma stood up and looked expectantly at Cleo. *It's time to really make this party happen!* she thought.

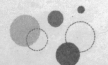
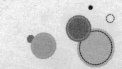

Chapter 14

After Miriam had walked out, Rikki felt pretty miserable. She didn't know where Emma and Cleo had disappeared to, and she didn't feel as if she had anything in common with the 'sleepover club', as she thought of them. She found a spare sleeping bag and curled up in the corner, clutching Emma's necklace in her hand. *I wonder who owned this first*, she thought. *Whoever she was, I'm not surprised she dropped it into the sea. It hasn't exactly brought good luck!*

When Emma and Cleo walked back into the lounge room, they were greeted with shouts of excitement and laughter. Everyone was giggling about Miriam and how she had overreacted. Some of them were still pondering the mystery of the exploding drinks containers. A couple of girls suggested that Emma's house was haunted,

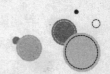

which made Cleo snort with laughter, picturing a ghostly mermaid … in a sleeping bag.

The girls had mopped up the liquid on the floor and wiped down the walls, ceiling and surfaces. The kitchen no longer looked as if a bomb had gone off in it. Emma was still going to have to explain a few blackcurrant stains, but she knew that her mum would expect one or two spillages. She thanked them all as they settled down cosily into their sleeping bags, grabbing piles of magazines and chattering about the latest celebrity stories. Caitlin was poring over a magazine poster, trying to decide which guy was cutest.

"That one," Alyssa insisted, pointing to a hunky male model.

"No way!" squealed Fiona. "I hate his tattoo!"

They all giggled and continued to argue.

Emma was about to join them when she saw Rikki on the other side of the room. She was sitting a little apart from the others, looking

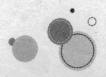

very thoughtful and serious. Emma nudged Cleo and nodded in Rikki's direction.

Emma and Cleo went to join their friend, wondering what was wrong. *I don't think I have ever seen Rikki look quite so solemn*, Emma thought. *I hope she's okay. Maybe she just really can't stand being at a sleepover any longer!*

Deep down, Rikki knew that her friends would believe her. But she was tense and nervous about telling them what had happened. She listened quietly while Cleo told her about her close shave in the closet, hoping that it would cheer her up. But even the thought of Cleo wrapped up in a sleeping bag didn't raise a flicker of a smile.

Finally, in a low voice, Rikki told them what Miriam had done. She described how Miriam had taken the necklace and what she had said when Rikki challenged her. Emma and Cleo were appalled when they heard the story, and

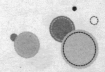

they were angry on Rikki's behalf when they heard what Miriam had said to her. To Rikki, that felt better and meant more than it would have done if the whole town had said they believed her. She handed the necklace to Emma, feeling instantly happier.

"Miriam's got some nerve, taking this," said Emma, feeling totally appalled.

"Should we tell everyone?" demanded Cleo.

"No point," said Rikki bitterly. "Like she said, it's my word against hers."

She's right, thought Emma sadly. *Miriam has loads of mean friends who would just spread horrible rumours about Rikki to get back at her. I just wish that there were something I could do to show everyone what a two-faced person Miriam really is.*

Cleo sighed and looked over at the other girls. They were shrieking with laughter as they gossiped and shared secrets. *I don't want to miss out on any more fun!* she thought.

"We should join the party," she said.

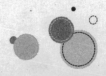

Emma nodded, glad to put Miriam out of her head. They were about to get to their feet when Rikki screwed up her face.

"I'm thinking … *not*," she said, knowing that her friends would understand. "It's not really my scene."

She looked down at the sleeping bag that she was wrapped in and winced. It had the words 'SLEEP OUT' embroidered on it in rainbow colours. *There are some places I'm just never going to fit in,* she admitted to herself, *and I am very pleased about it!*

Emma and Cleo smiled at her, understanding completely. They too had found it difficult to imagine Rikki enjoying a full-on sleepover party.

I wish she'd stay, thought Emma, *but I'm not going to force her to do anything. As if I could!*

Rikki was about to say goodbye when there was a shout from the girls in the other corner.

"Hey Emma," called Caitlin. "Which guy in the swimming team's got the cutest legs?"

There was a buzz of interest and Emma thought for a second, mentally running through all the guys she had trained alongside.

"Um … Sam," she declared.

"No way!" said Rikki at once, staring at her as if she were crazy. "*Joshua* – hottie."

Cleo grinned at Rikki and exchanged a knowing glance with Emma. Maybe this was something Rikki could understand after all!

"Come on," said Ashleigh. "We're building the perfect guy out of the guys on the swimming team."

Rikki looked at them in surprise. *This is the first time all night that any of these girls has sounded vaguely normal*, she thought. *And that idea sounds … kind of cool!*

"What did you reckon, Rikki?" asked Emma, as if she had read her mind. "That we spend our whole time talking about negative splits?"

Rikki's eyes sparkled with laughter as she

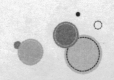

looked at Emma.

"There might be something normal about these chicks after all," she admitted.

She stood up and gathered her rainbow-coloured, 'SLEEP OUT' sleeping bag around herself. Then she bunny-hopped over to join the other girls.

Cleo looked at Emma, highly amused. But Emma's face was suddenly serious again. She held out the beautiful necklace.

"This might be safer with you," she said.

"With me?" repeated Cleo, shaking her head. "*You* found it ..."

"And I nearly managed to get it stolen," Emma added. "I know how much you like it. Here."

She leaned forward and put the necklace into Cleo's hand.

"You sure?" asked Cleo.

Emma smiled and glanced around the room. No one was listening. She bent towards Cleo

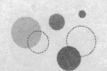

and spoke in a soft voice.

"Anyone who can hide a mermaid tail in the middle of a party ... has got what it takes to look after that," she said.

Cleo grinned ... and accepted the necklace.

"Come on," said Emma, standing up.

They went over to join the others, who had moved on from picking features from the swimming team and were now choosing parts of celebrities instead. Emma plumped down on a pillow next to Rikki, who looked at her and grinned.

"What about him?" Fiona was asking, pointing to a picture in her magazine.

"His eyes," agreed Alyssa.

Emma and Cleo settled down happily. Tonight, they could forget all about being mermaids. Tonight, they were just ordinary girls again.

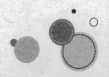

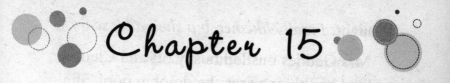

Chapter 15

It was a brand-new day at the Marine Park. Dolphins dived, leapt and played together. The monorail powered by. Early visitors strolled through the park, gasping at the amazing animals and enjoying the peace of the early morning.

Cleo walked out of the staff area into the dolphin enclosure. She was carrying two shiny buckets full of fish and squid, and she now had two towels tucked into the back of her apron.

Mrs Geddes walked past her and gave her a huge smile.

"Keep up the good work, Cleo," she said, patting her on the shoulder. "You're really starting to fit in around here."

"Thanks, Mrs Geddes," said Cleo, feeling really proud.

Mrs Geddes is a bit like a strict teacher, she

thought. *I really like her, but she's a bit scary.*

Mrs Geddes bustled busily off and Cleo walked briskly towards the dolphin pool. She knew that they would be hungry for their breakfast, and she didn't want to keep them waiting. But then she saw something that made her stop and stare. Her blood seemed to tingle in her veins as she took in the sight.

A woman was standing alone on the little wooden bridge that stretched over the dolphin pool. She had her back to Cleo, but there was no mistaking that long, golden hair, flowing down her back in two long coils. It was the same, mysterious woman who had seemed to know so much about Cleo.

Cleo put down her buckets of fish. *I had forgotten all about her!* she realized in amazement. *I was so caught up with Emma's party – and then the accident. She just went totally out of my head!*

Cleo thought for a moment and then walked

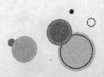

swiftly towards the woman. For once she didn't even notice the dolphins, who were clicking impatiently, waiting for their food. All her attention was focused on the woman who was standing so quiet and still.

As she reached her, the woman turned to her with a smile, almost as if she had sensed her coming. But her expression of welcome changed to one of shock when she saw the necklace around Cleo's neck.

"You found it in the pool, didn't you?" she asked at once. "On Mako Island."

Her voice was heavy with emotion. Cleo didn't know what to say. She had never met anyone like this before. There had been no introduction; there was no 'Good morning' or 'How are you?'; this unusual lady talked as if she had known Cleo all her life.

"That's where Gracie lost it," she went on in a hushed tone. "Fifty years ago."

She reached out and touched the locket. Cleo was totally stunned. *She knows about the*

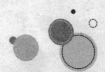

pool! she thought, her head in a whirl. *She knows about the necklace. Does that mean that she's like us? Does it mean she's …*

"So …" Cleo stammered, struggling to string her words together. "You mean … you're …"

The lady seemed to be lost in a dream … or in her memories. Her eyes were shining with tears as she stroked the locket. Then she seemed to pull herself back into the present. A youthful expression of amusement came over her face.

"I'm 65 years old, yes," she said quickly. "But I don't look any more than 68, right?"

She laughed as Cleo shook her head.

"That's not what I meant–" Cleo said.

"I know what you mean," said the woman, stroking Cleo's arm kindly. "Even if you don't. What's your name again?"

"Cleo," she said. *I'm sure I never told her my name in the first place*, she thought.

The woman looked deep into her eyes. Cleo

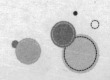

looked back, fascinated by how blue and vibrant the woman's eyes were.

"You've got *spirit*, Cleo," said the woman, almost as if she were reading her thoughts and feelings. "Enjoy it. Enjoy it all you can."

Cleo nodded as the woman gripped her arm tighter, emphasizing each word with a squeeze.

"You and your friends ..." she said, closing her eyes and touching the necklace again, "... maybe *you'll* be all right ... eventually."

Cleo looked out over the dolphin pool, wondering what she meant. She was so involved in her thoughts that she barely noticed the woman slip away and leave the bridge. Cleo felt so confused and surprised that she could barely move or speak. Then she realized that the woman was about to vanish – *again*.

"*Wait*!" Cleo exclaimed. "Don't go!"

The woman was on the path that led out of the Marine Park. She turned for a moment and gave Cleo an enigmatic smile. But she didn't say another word.

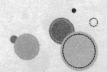

"What do you mean?" Cleo pleaded, as she turned and kept walking.

It was no use. She had a million questions to ask ... but the mysterious woman had disappeared again.

Cleo walked back to her buckets of fish, lost in thought. Whoever this woman was, she obviously knew much more about what was happening than Cleo and her friends did. The dolphins clicked and squeaked noisily as Cleo picked up the buckets and walked to the edge of the pool with them.

Next time I see her, I'm just going to have to hold on to her and call Rikki and Emma! she thought, dramatically. *She has answers, and that's exactly what we need! That is, if there is a next time.*

But something told Cleo that she hadn't seen the last of the lady. She picked up a fish with her tongs and threw it into the mouth of a hungry dolphin. She had a funny feeling that this was just the start of their adventures.

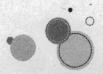